There are many versions of this classic tale. In the tradition of the storyteller, each one is uniquely different.

Library of Congress Cataloging-in-Publication Data

José, Eduard.
   [Aventuras de Till Eulenspiegel.   English]
   Till Eulenspiegel's merry pranks / illustration,
Francesc Rovira ; adaptation, Eduard José ; retold
by Janet Riehecky.
      p. cm. — (A Classic tale)
   Translation of: Aventuras de Till Eulenspiegel.
   Summary: A retelling of the adventures of the
prankster who traveled all over medieval Germany
playing jokes on people and swindling the unwary.
   ISBN 0-89565-475-X
   [1. Folklore—Germany.]   I. Rovira, Francesc,
ill.   II. Riehecky, Janet, 1953-   .
III. Eulenspiegel (Satire)   IV. Title.   V. Series.
PZ8.1.J75Ti   1988
398.2'2'0943—dc19 [E]   88-36794   CIP AC

© 1988 Parramón Ediciones, S. A.
Printed in Spain
© Alexander Publishers' Marketing
and The Child's World, Inc.: English
edition, 1988.

A CLASSIC TALE

Till Eulenspiegel's Merry Pranks

Illustration: Francesc Rovira

Adaptation: Isidro Sánchez

Retold by Janet Riehecky

The Child's World, Inc.

Once upon a time there lived a man named Till Eulenspiegel. He was a carefree fellow who loved to laugh. Now there's nothing wrong with laughter—except that Till liked best to laugh at other people. He traveled the countryside, playing practical jokes. His favorite pastime was making others look foolish.

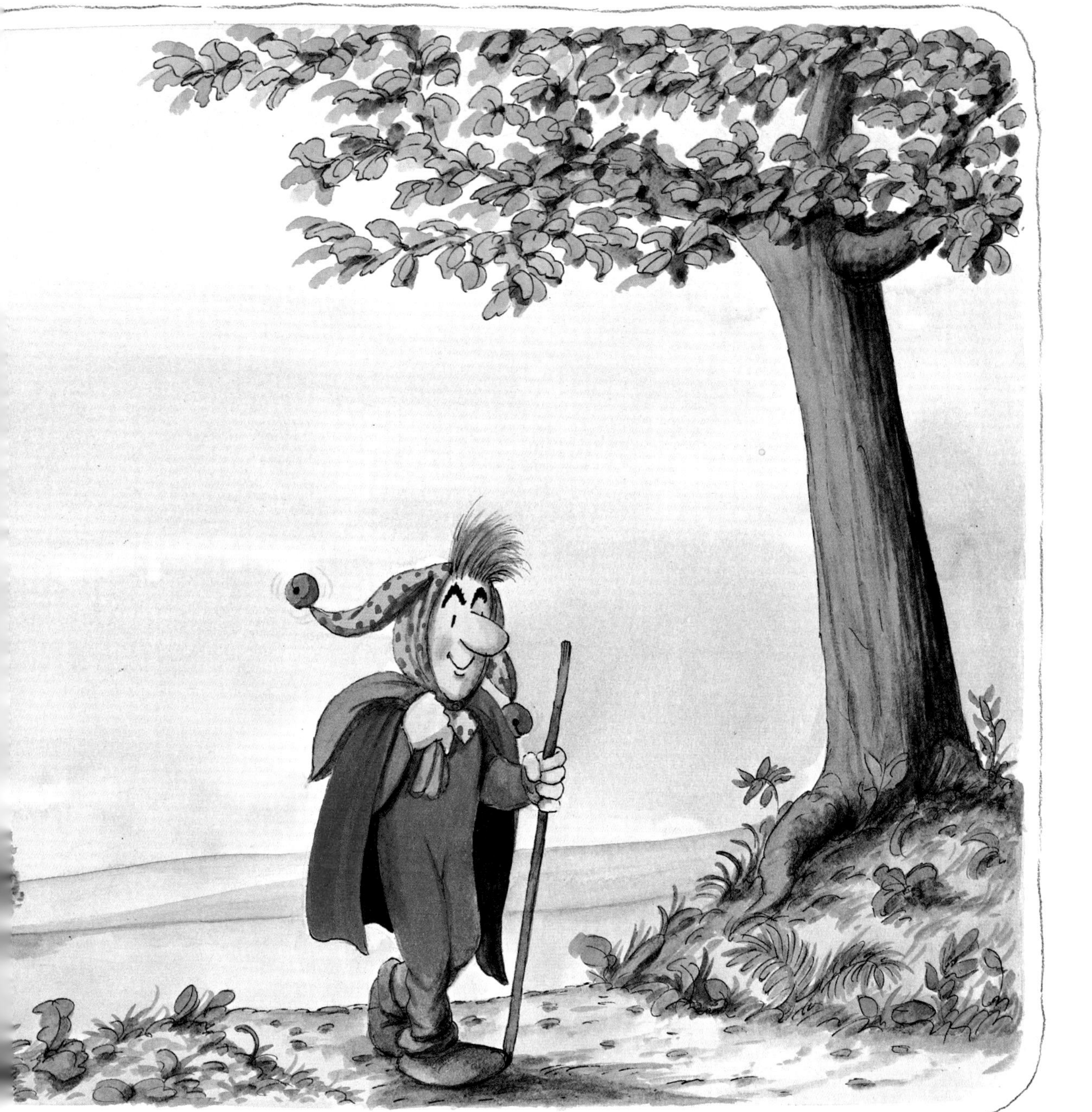

Perhaps Till's love of practical jokes began when he was a child. He was born in a village that was so small it didn't have its own market. When it was time to shop, Till's family had to travel to the next village.

One day as the family crossed a small bridge returning home, Till's nurse slipped. Her shoe went flying one way, and poor Till went flying the other. *Splat!* Till landed in the muddy creek

There was an anxious moment while Till's mother made sure Till wasn't hurt. Then everyone burst into laughter. Till was a muddy mess. And later on he had to take a bath when it wasn't even Saturday! He never forgot what happened that day. Till had learned that the misfortunes of others could make people laugh. And he was determined that never again would he be the one people laughed at.

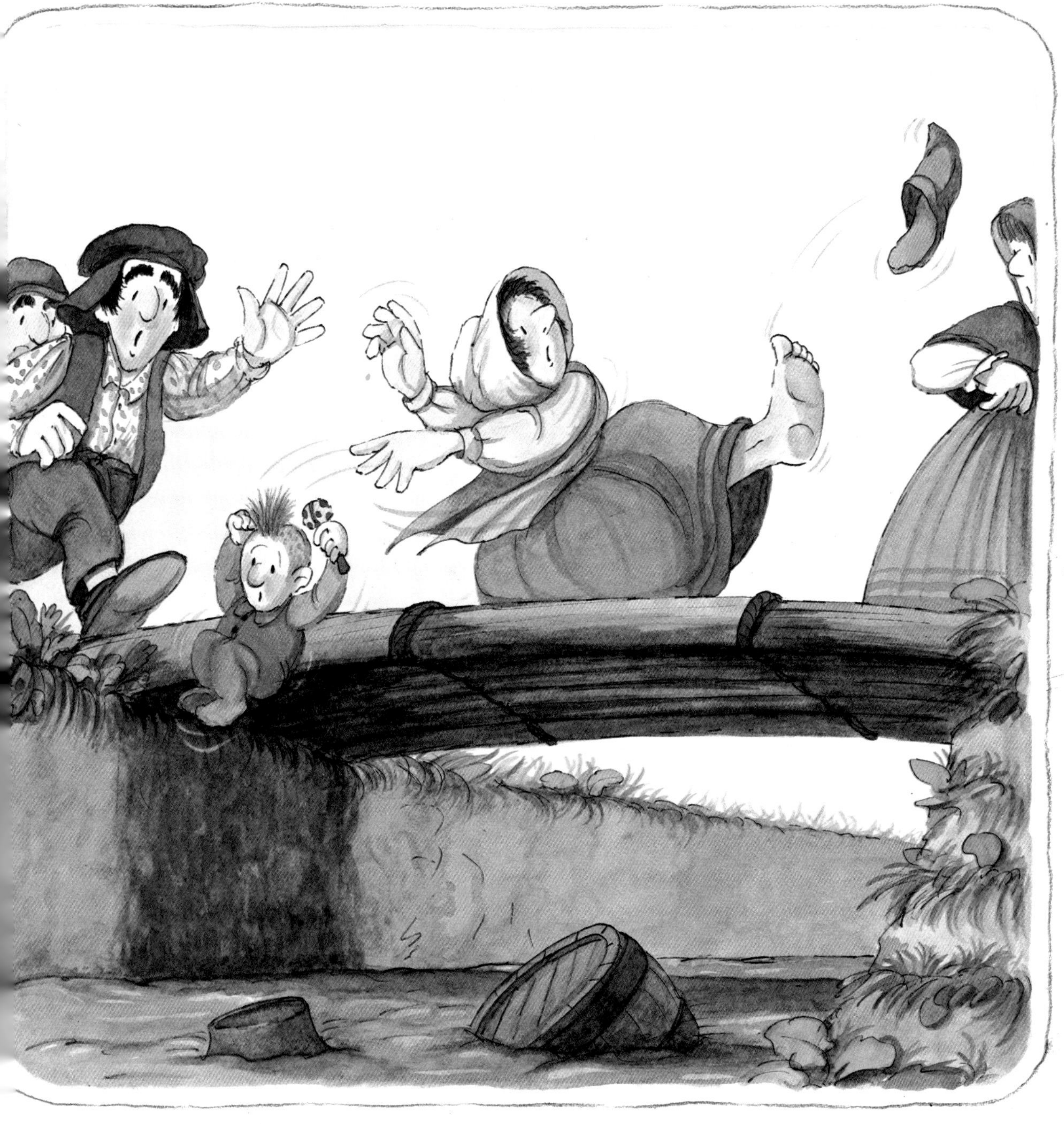

When he grew up, Till decided not to get a job unless he really had to. And his goal was to play as many tricks on as many people as he could—without getting caught.

One day Till stretched a long rope from his bedroom window to the house across the street. Then he called to his neighbors, "I'll bet all of you that I can walk across that tightrope carrying one shoe from each of you on my back."

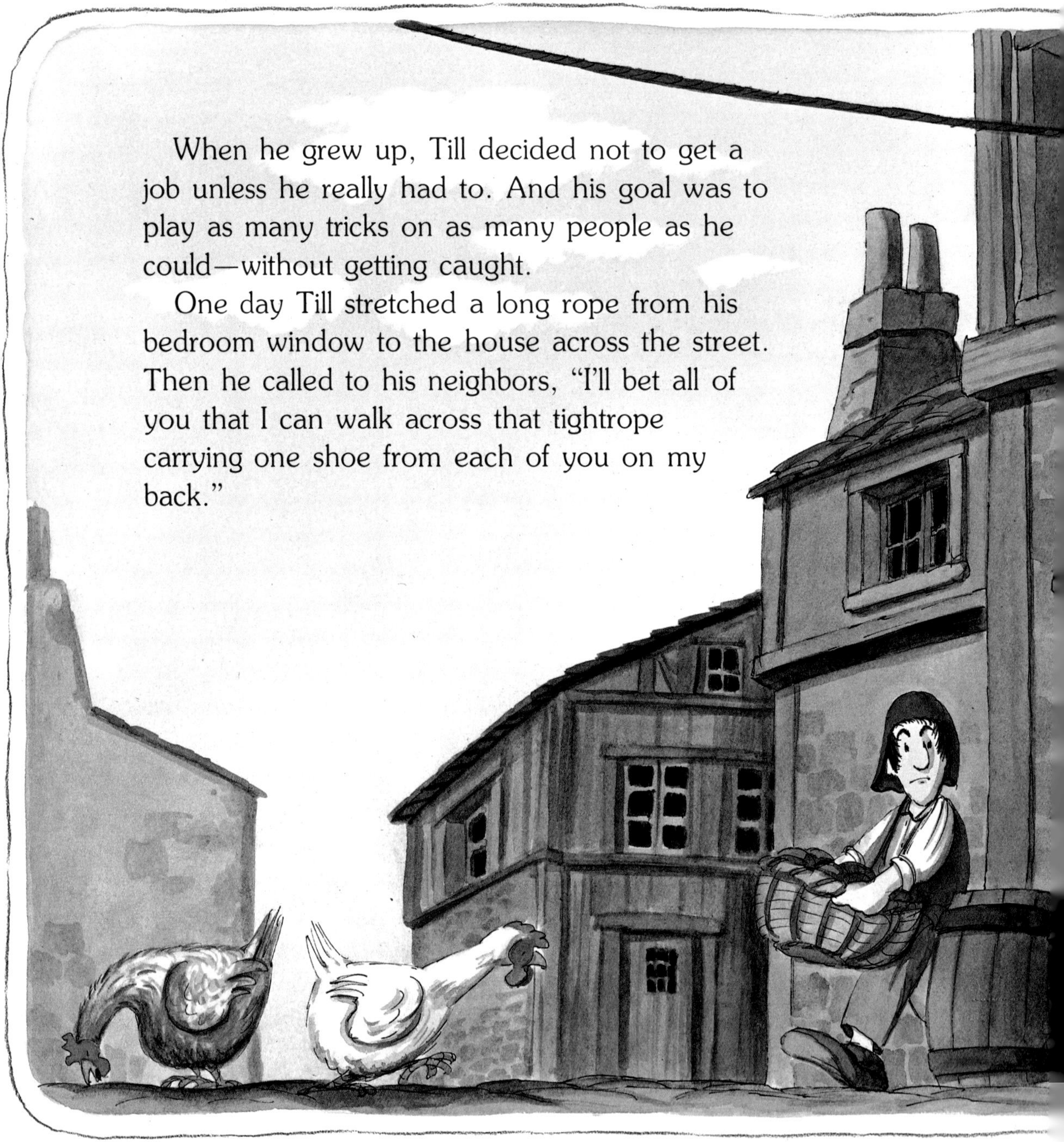

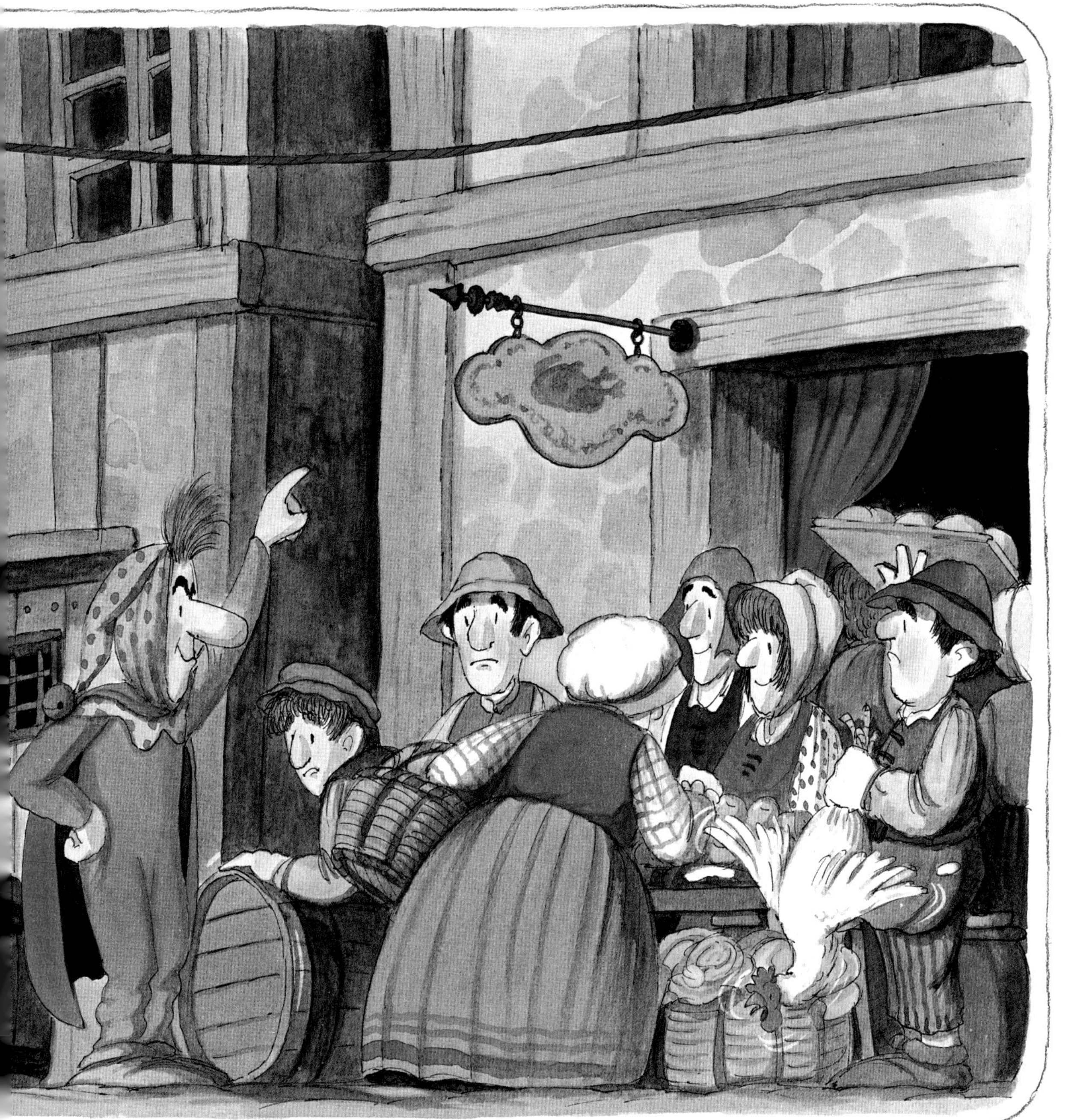

"Sure," said some.

"Not a chance!" said some others, who knew Till too well.

Most of the neighbors joined in the game. They each took off a shoe and gave it to him. Till wrapped all the shoes in a blanket. Then he climbed onto the rope and took a few steps. Till got halfway across the rope. Then, suddenly, he whipped open the blanket and scattered all the shoes down onto the people below.

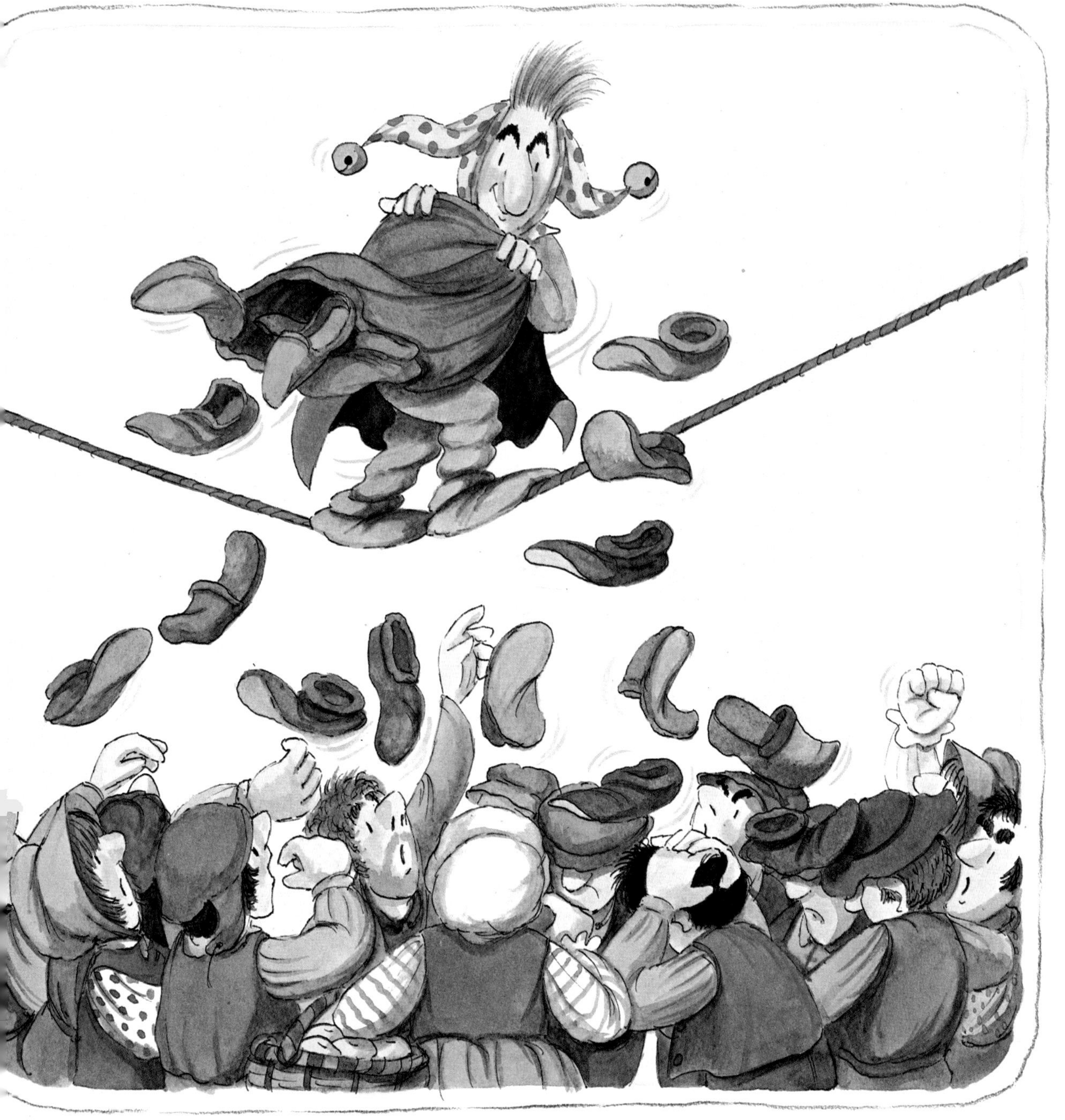

First everyone ducked, trying not to be hit by a flying shoe. Then they scrambled, trying to find their shoes.

"Hey! That's mine!" shouted one man, pulling at a boot.

"No, it isn't! It's mine!" shouted another, tugging at the same boot. Soon the confusion became an argument, and the argument became a fight. The whole village was in the street swapping punches—and Till Eulenspiegel sat in his window, doubled over with laughter.

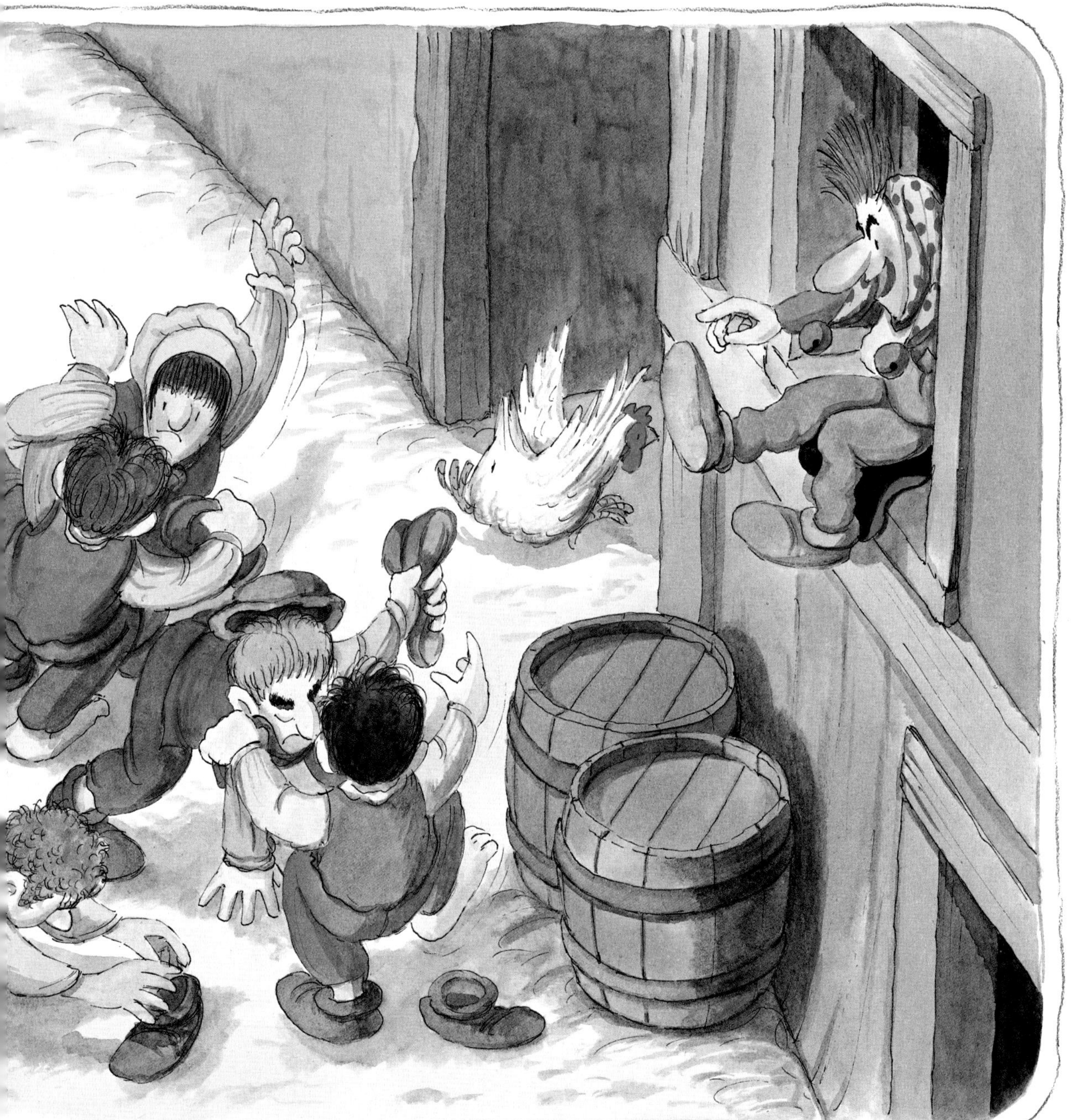

Because of his strange sense of humor, Till could be a bad person to give an important job.

For instance, in one city he offered his services to Count Van Anhalt. The count hired him to be a lookout. A gang of bandits had been raiding the castle grounds, and Till was supposed to stand on the castle tower and sound the alarm if he saw the bandits approaching.

Unfortunately, not only could Till see the countryside from the tower, he could also see the castle yard where the count and his knights ate their dinner. Each night he watched them have a lavish feast. And then each night when he got off duty, he was served only a small bowl of porridge.

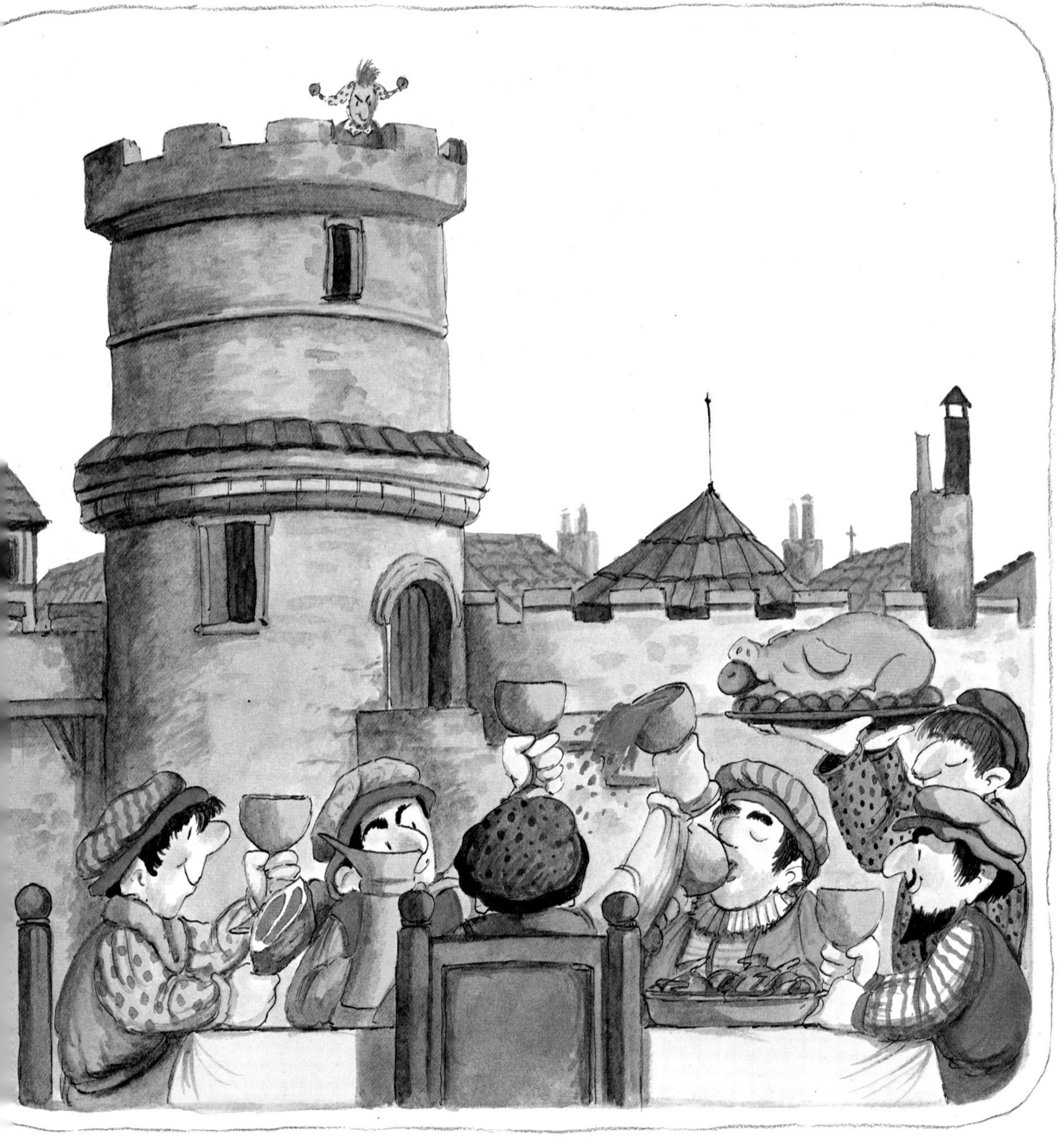

One day as Till stood his post, the bandits suddenly roared across the fields. They came right up to the castle gates. There they rounded up all the cattle and sheep and set fire to the barns. Till stood watching, but he didn't sound the alarm.

Finally, one of the farmhands ran to the castle. He found the count and cried out, "The bandits are attacking!" Quickly, Count Van Anhalt and his knights jumped on their horses and set off in pursuit. But it was too late.

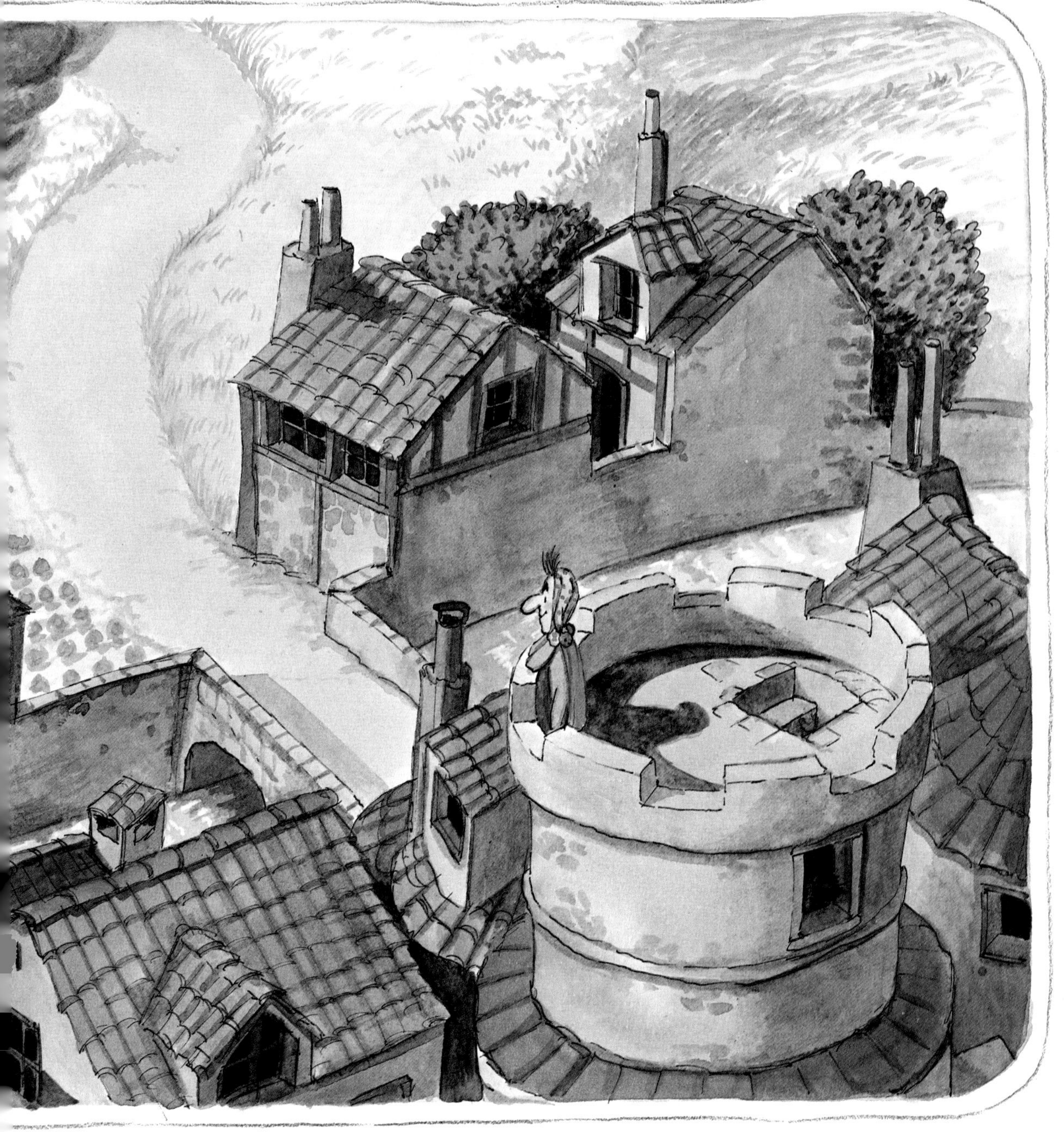

"You numbskull!" the count shouted at Till when they returned. "Why didn't you sound the alarm?"

"It is difficult to sound the alarm with a stomach full of cobwebs," Till replied.

During the next few days, the count and his knights searched the countryside. Eventually, they found the bandits and managed to steal back the stolen cattle and sheep. When they returned to the castle, the count ordered several of the beasts to be roasted to celebrate the victory.

High up in the tower, Till smelled the delicious roasting meat. He made a quick decision. He snatched his horn and blew the alarm.

The count and his knights leaped up from their feast, flung on their armor, and galloped out of the castle.

As soon as they were gone, Till slipped from his post. Quickly, he shoveled up all the meat he could carry from the count's feast. Then he climbed back up to his post and stuffed himself until he was ready to burst.

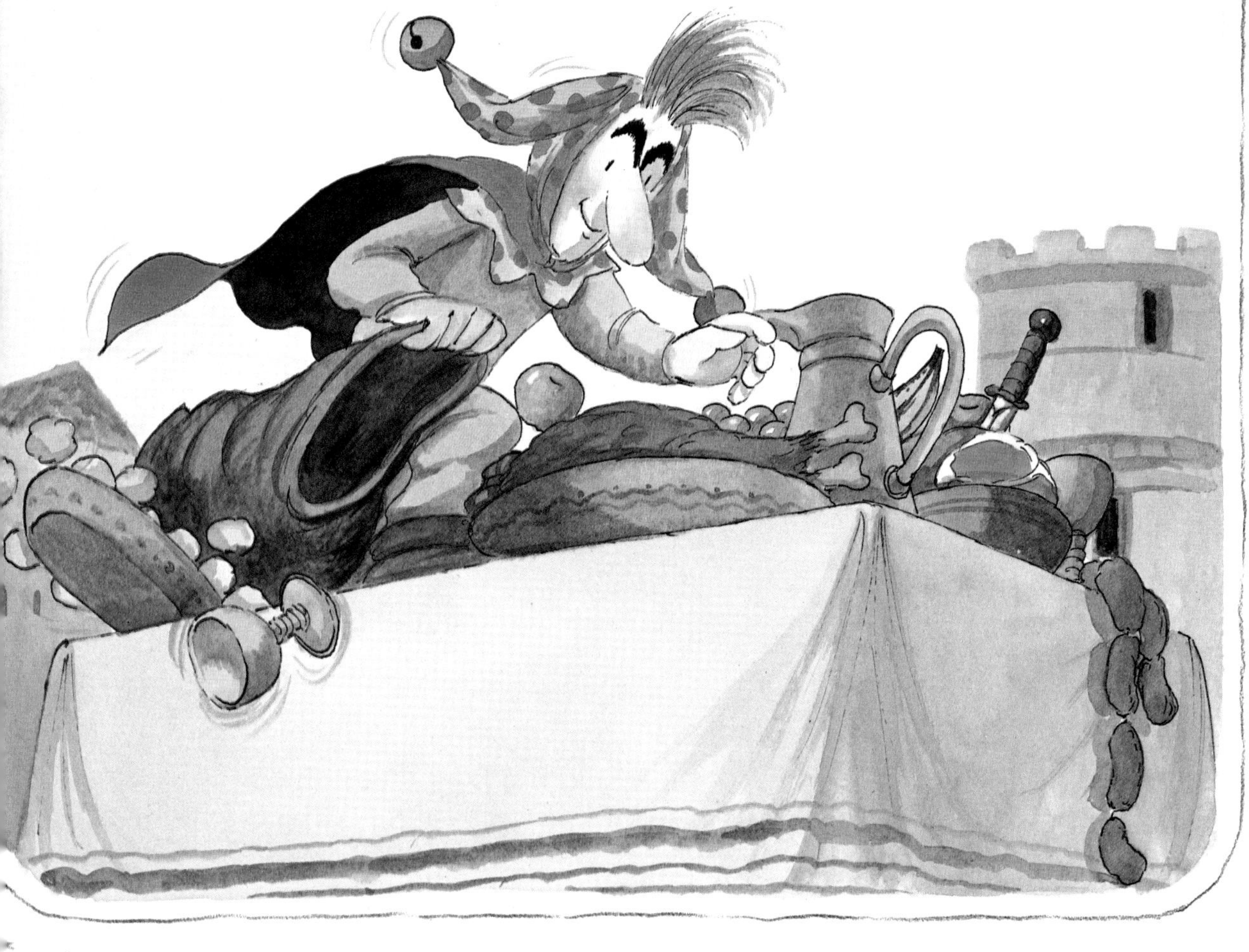

Soon the count and his knights galloped back to the castle. They had found no trace of the bandits. The count climbed up to the tower, his face purple with rage. "Have you gone out of your mind?" he screamed at Till. "When the bandits came, you stood there as if nothing were happening. And now that there isn't an enemy in sight, you sound the alarm!"

"Blame it on hunger," answered Till. "With an empty stomach, you see ghosts all over the place." With that, Till fell into fits of laughter.

The count was so angry, he ordered Till to leave his castle immediately and never come back.

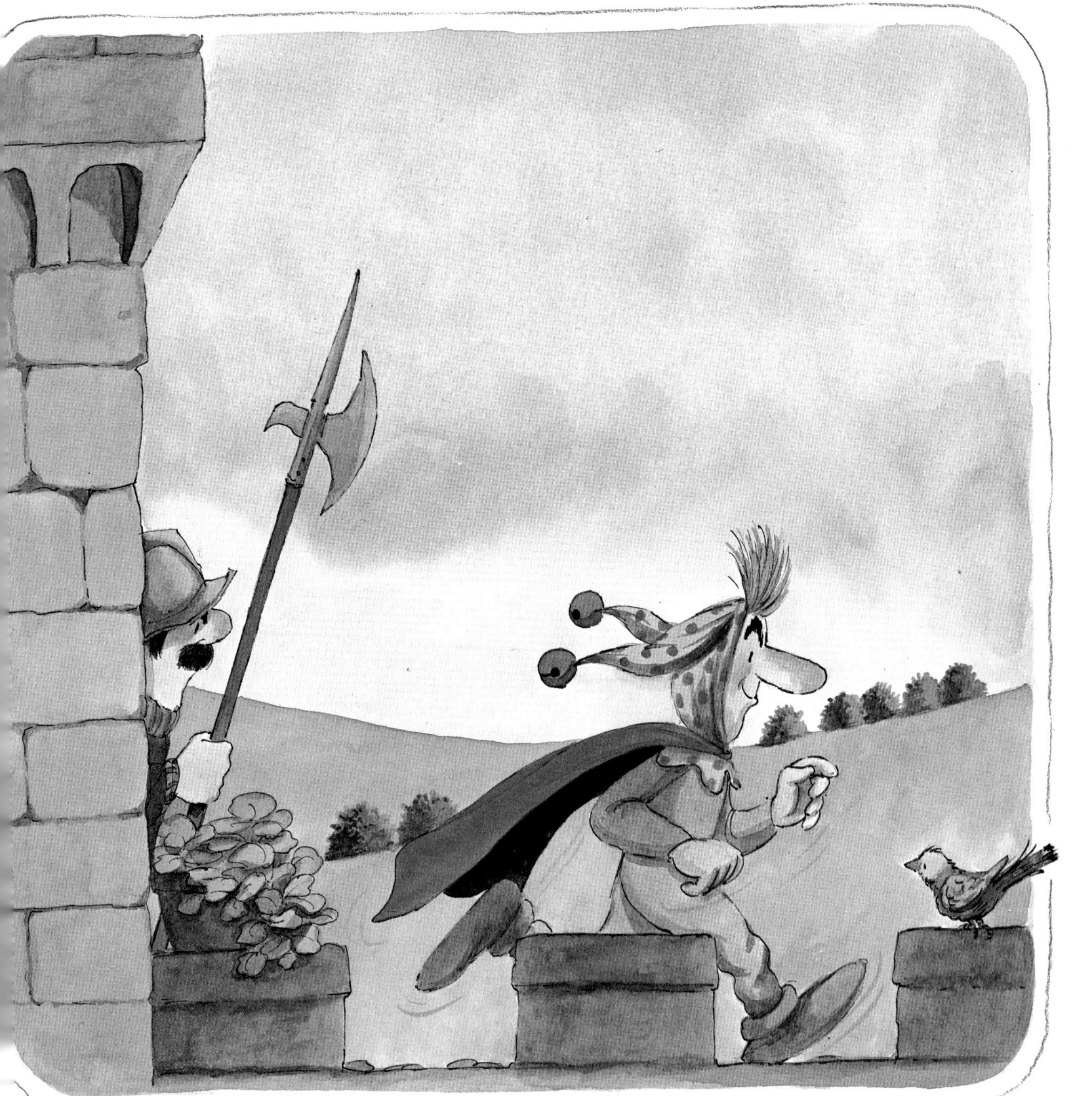

Soon after that, Till decided he should move on to a new town. (You can imagine why.) He headed for the village of Erfurt. Once again, he got a great idea for a practical joke. He went to the university and called together all the professors.

"Gentlemen," he said to them, "I have traveled a great distance to share with you an amazing discovery I have made. I have perfected a method of teaching that can even teach a donkey to read!"

The professors gasped in amazement. "Tell us more!" they begged.

"I would like to," Till replied. "But something so marvelous cannot be taught for free. I shall share my discovery for $200."

The professors quickly agreed. Such a wonderful discovery could not be passed over.

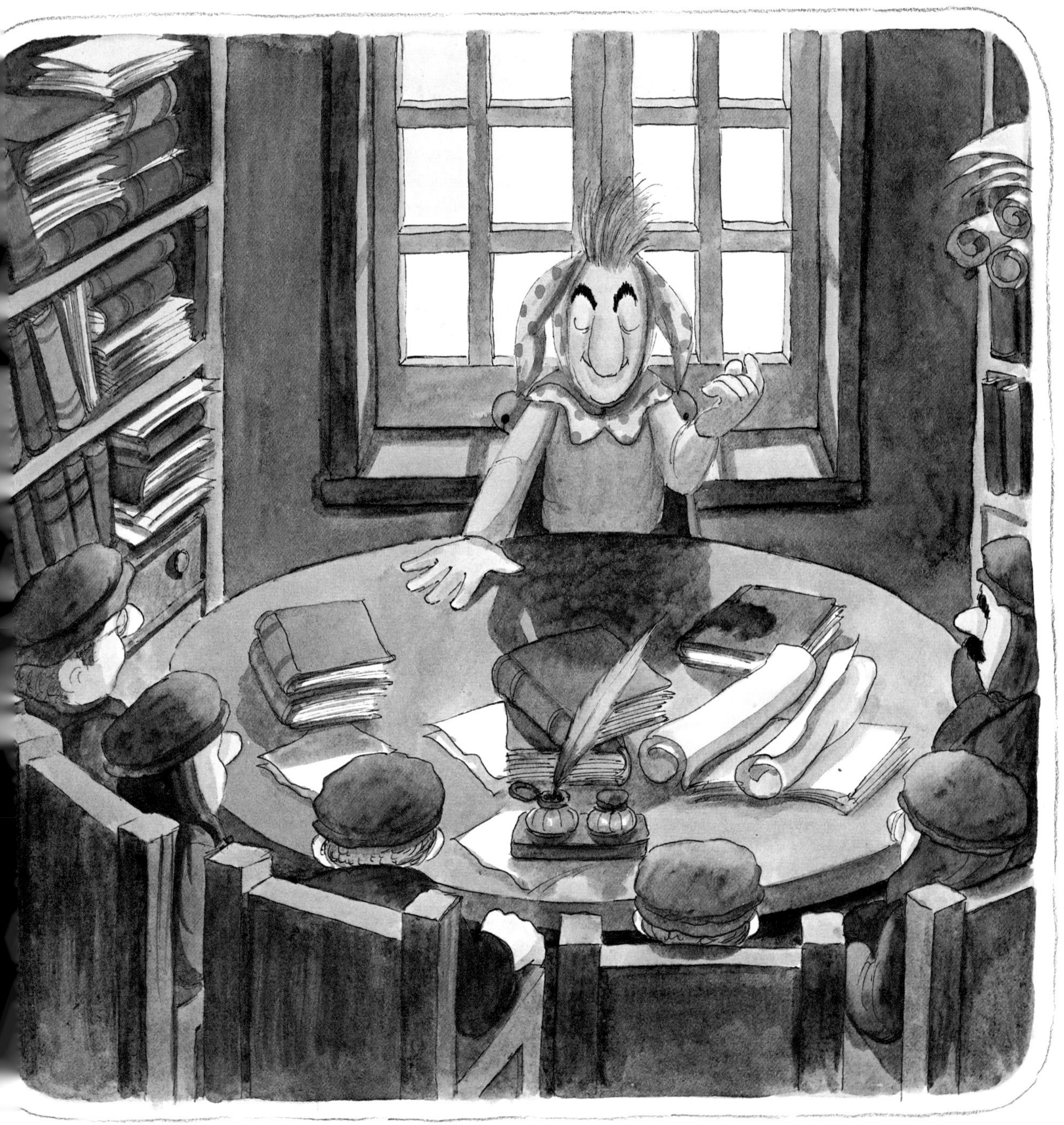

The next day Till brought an old, bony, flea-ridden donkey into the university library. He began his demonstration.

"Gentlemen, observe," he began proudly. He walked over to the donkey and pulled its tail.

"Ee-oo!" brayed the donkey.

"You see my amazing success," said Till. "Already this creature has learned the letters 'e' and 'o.' Tomorrow I will start teaching him 'a' and 'i.'"

The professors turned red with anger. For all their knowledge, they had fallen for a silly trick.

"We demand our money back!" they cried. But Till had already slipped out the window, laughing hilariously.

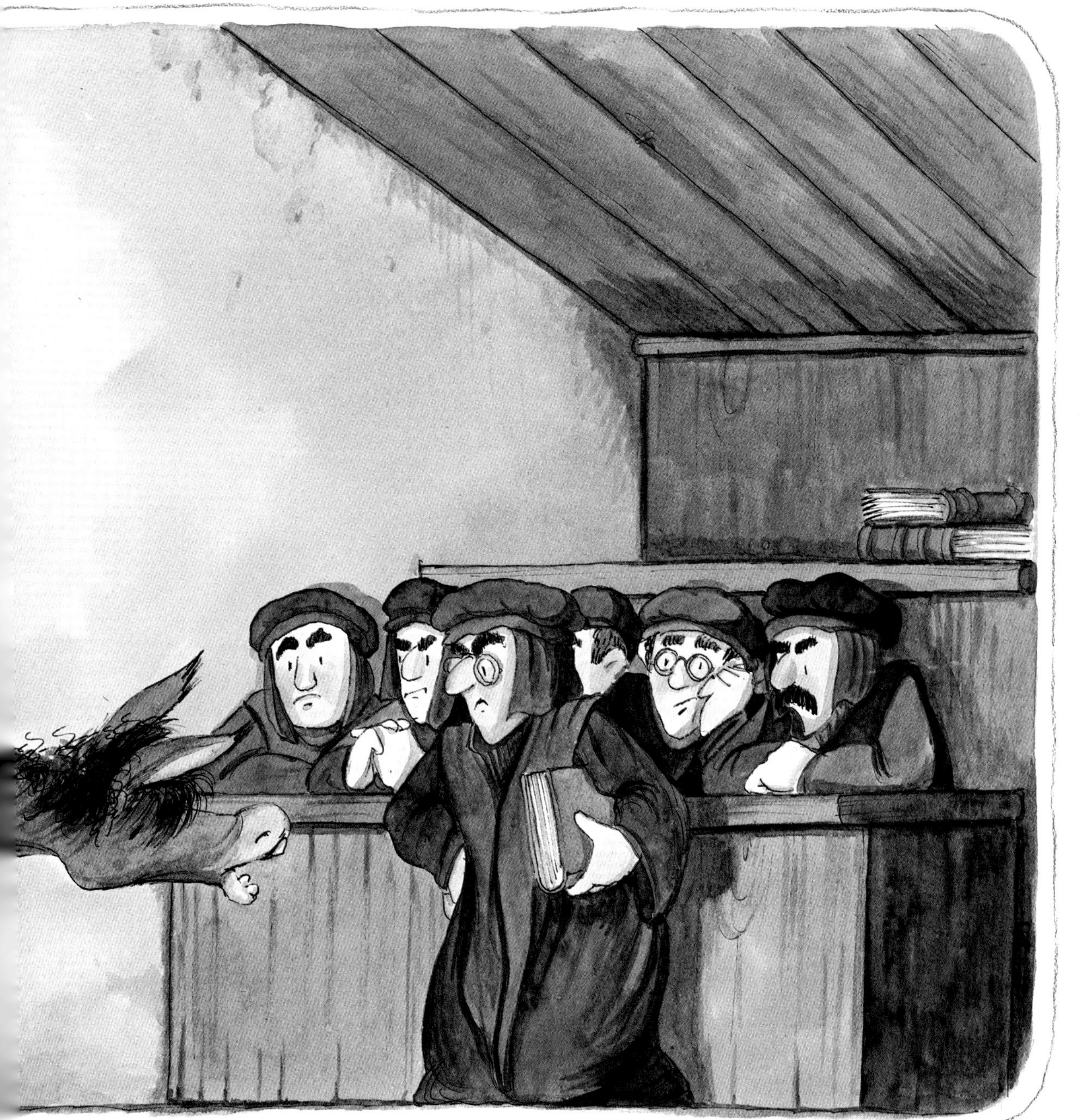

In the next city that Till visited, he made enemies once again. The count there swore revenge on the prankster for playing so many nasty tricks.

"If you ever set foot on my soil again, I'll have you skinned alive!" cried the count.

Till was not about to leave a challenge like that unanswered. So he went and bought a

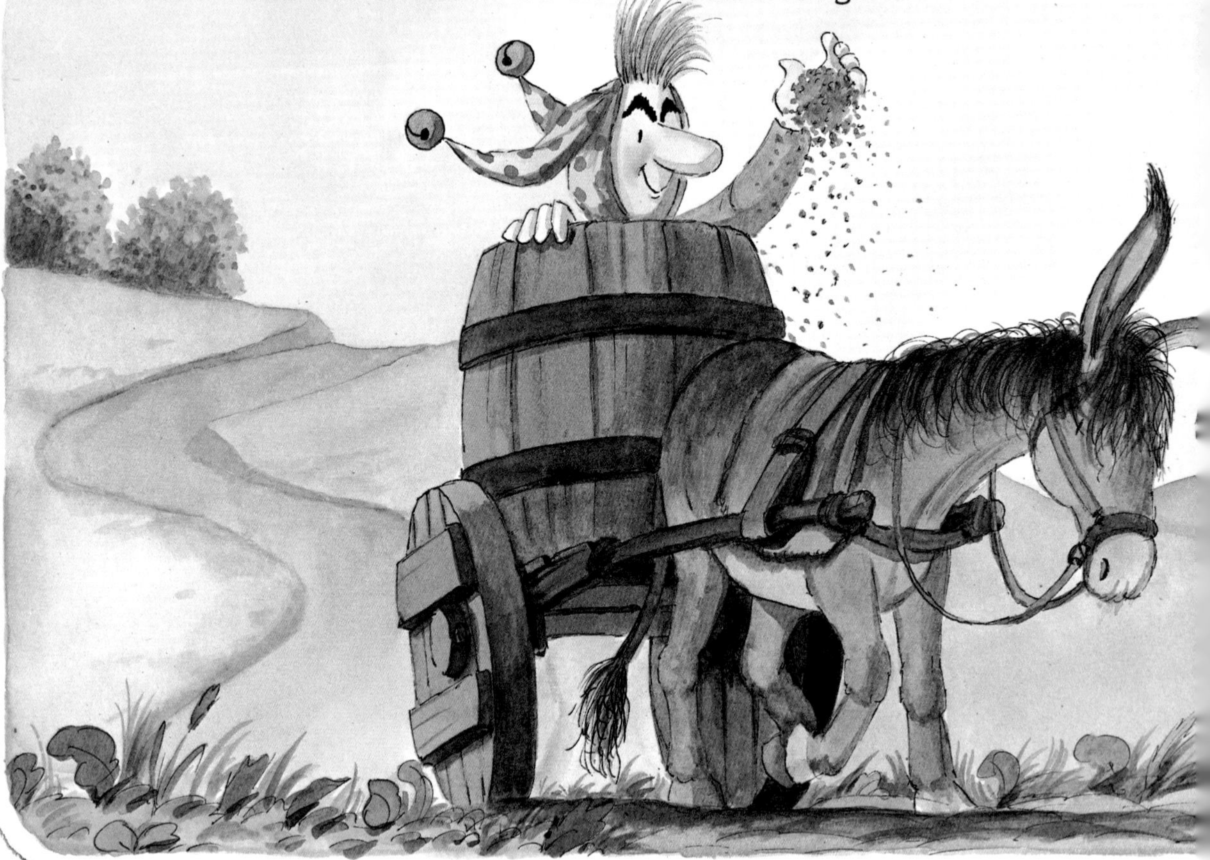

barrel of soil. He loaded it on a cart and climbed in, leaving just his head sticking out. Then he returned to the count's castle.

"You can't say I'm on your soil!" Till called out as he paraded proudly in front of the count. "I paid for this soil, and now it belongs to me!"

The count sputtered with rage, but Till just laughed.

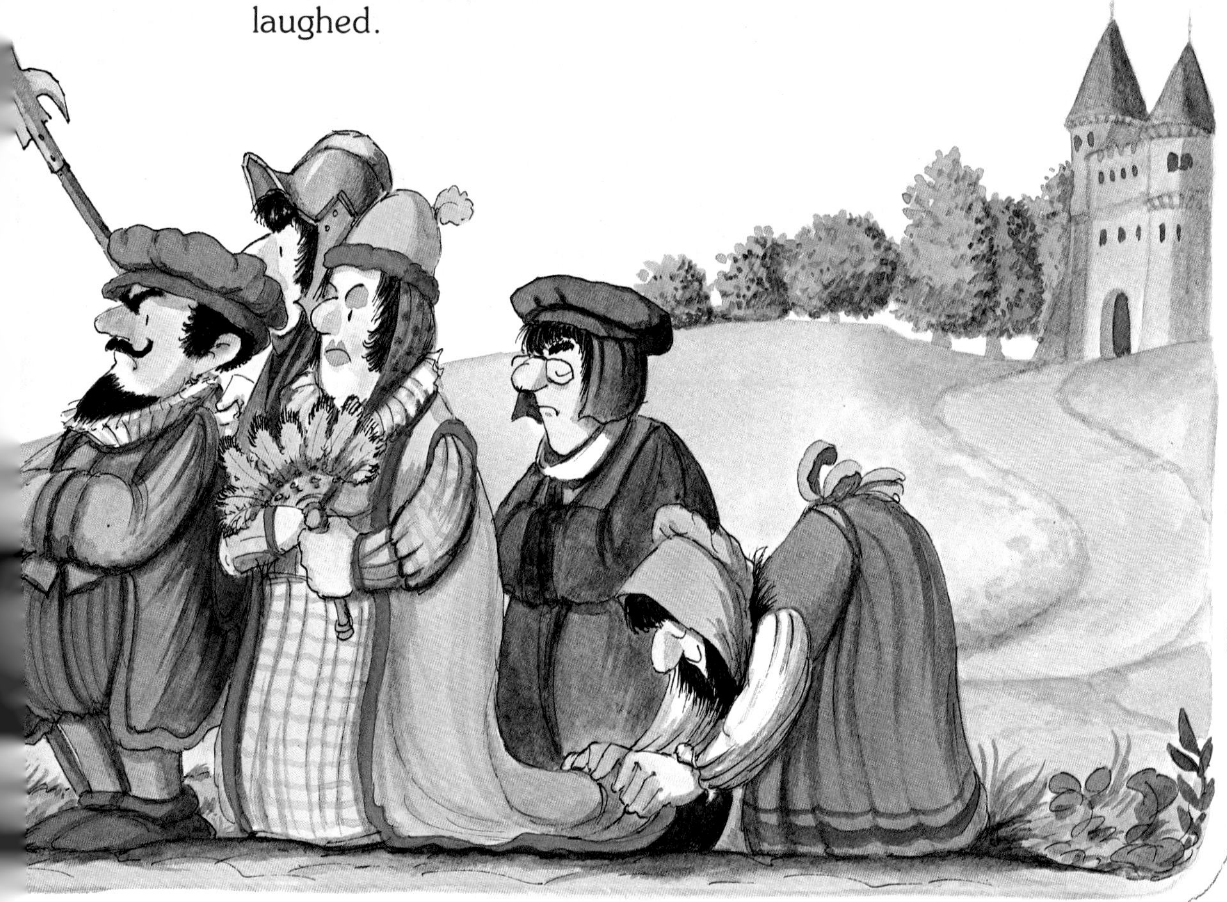

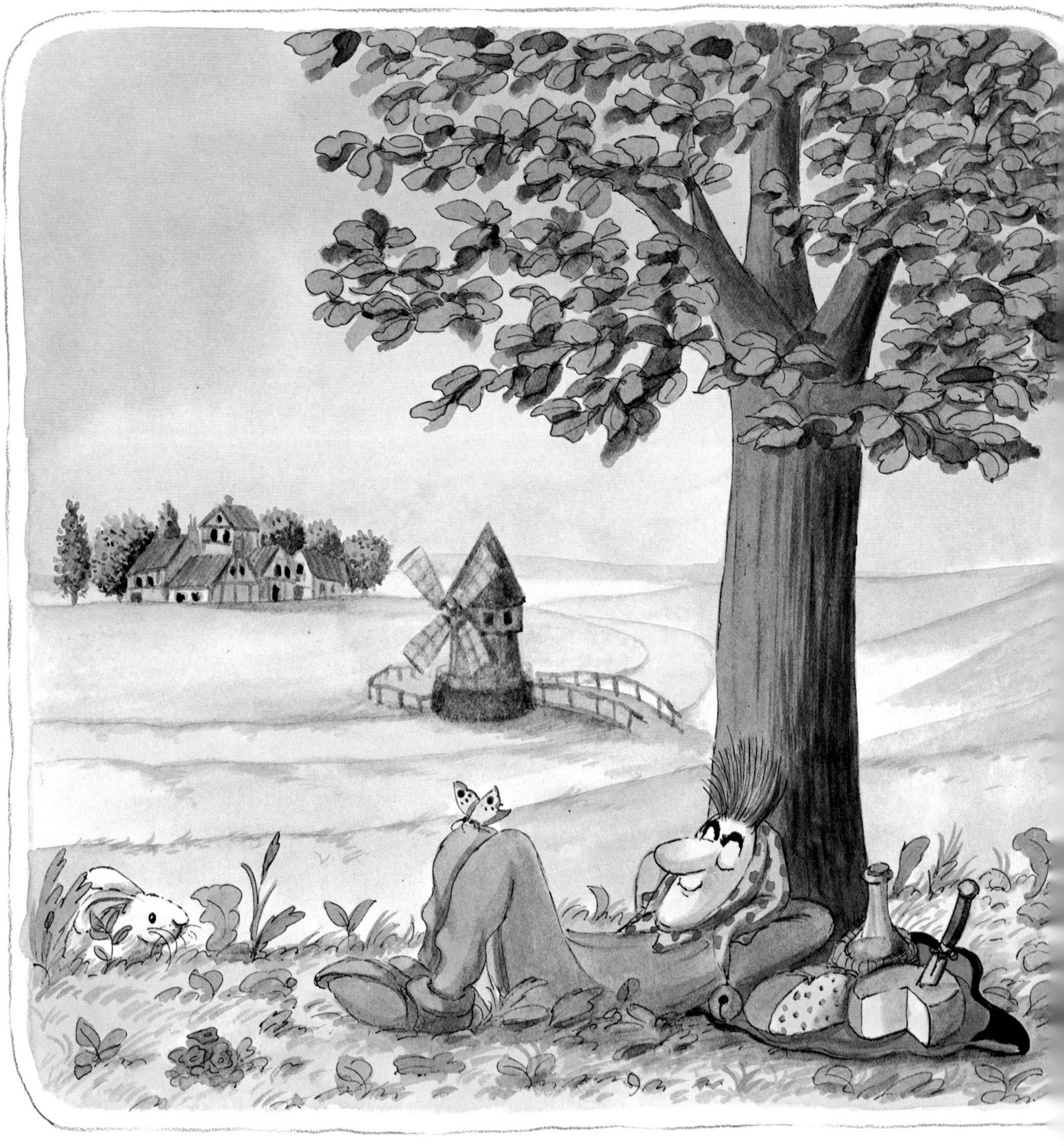

Till wandered the countryside for many years. His adventures could fill a five-thousand page book. Life was an amusing game for him, and each new day was an exciting challenge. Till played many a trick on the people he met. But even his victims sometimes had to smile at Till's outrageous jokes and their own foolishness. No one ever forgot meeting Till Eulenspiegel.